# Kathleen Bullock

# The Rabbits Are Coming!

SIMON & SCHUSTER BOOKS FOR YOUNG READERS
Published by Simon & Schuster
New York • London • Toronto • Sydney • Tokyo • Singapore

SIMON & SCHUSTER BOOKS FOR YOUNG READERS
Simon & Schuster Building, Rockefeller Center
1230 Avenue of the Americas, New York, New York 10020

Designed by Vicki Kalajian
Manufactured in the United States of America

10   9   8   7   6   5   4   3   2   1

Library of Congress Cataloging-in-Publication Data

Bullock, Kathleen, 1946-
The rabbits are coming! / by Kathleen Bullock.
p.   cm.   Summary: Rabbits bearing balloons frolic
through a house, causing much consternation among
its human occupants.   [1. Rabbits—Fiction.   2. Balloons—
Fiction.   3. Stories without words.]   I. Title.
PZ7.B9144Rab   1991   [E]—dc20   90-49830

ISBN 0-671-72963-2

This book is for these little bunnies:
Alison, Kaetlyn, Eve, Maggie and
Bucky, Kailey and Brenden, Morgan
and Taylor, Kevin, Thomas and Pierre.
Also: Alex, Bianca, Jake, Luke, Emily,
Clare and Mandy and Mary.

—K.B.